D1410180

The
Troublesome Pig

A Nursery Tale retold
and illustrated by Priscilla Lamont

Crown Publishers, Inc.   New York

Published in 1985 in the United States of America
by Crown Publishers, Inc.,
One Park Avenue, New York, New York 10016
Originally published in Great Britain by Hamish Hamilton Children's Books,
Garden House, 57-59 Long Acre, London WC2E 9JZ
Typeset in Great Britain by Ampersand Co. Ltd.
Originated and printed in Italy by Arnoldo Mondadori Editore, Verona

Library of Congress Cataloging in Publication Data
Lamont, Priscilla.
The troublesome pig.
Summary: An old woman does a lot of pleading with
a variety of creatures before she gets her pig over
the stile so they can get home that night.
[1. Folklore] I. Title.
PZ8.1.L197Tr 1985   398.2′452 [E]   84-7717
ISBN 0-517-55546-8
10 9 8 7 6 5 4 3 2 1
First American Edition

At the Mumbleton Monday Market, an old woman
bought a pig. "A fine pig that," said the farmer.
"It had better be," said the old woman. "It costs enough."

The old woman and her new pig set off for home.
Before long they reached a stile.

The old woman pushed

and she pulled

but try as she might, she could not
get the pig over that stile.

"Some fine pig you are," said the old woman.
And she went down the path until she met a dog.

"Please dog," she said,
"Bite my pig,
Then he'll jump over the stile,
And we shall get home tonight."
But would the dog bite the pig?

HE WOULD NOT.

"Well I never did," said the old woman.
Farther along the path she found a stick.

"Please stick," she said, "beat dog,
Then dog will bite pig,
The pig will jump over the stile,
And we shall get home tonight."
But would the stick beat the dog?

IT WOULD NOT.

"This won't do," said the old woman, rather put out.
So she went down the path until she found a fire.

"Please fire, burn stick," she said.
"Then stick will beat dog,
Dog will bite pig,
The pig will jump over the stile,
And we shall get home tonight."
But would the fire burn the stick?

IT WOULD NOT.

"That's got me quite hot under the collar,"
the old woman puffed as she thought of the
long walk home. But soon she came to a stream.

She said a little breathlessly,
"Please water, quench fire,
Then fire will burn stick,
Stick will beat dog,
Dog will bite pig,
The pig will jump over the stile,
And we shall get home tonight."
But would the water quench the fire?

IT WOULD NOT.

"This is a pretty kettle of fish," sighed the old woman,
which reminded her that it was almost time for tea.
On down the path she went until she found a horse.

"Please horse," she said,
"Drink water,
Then water will quench fire,
Fire will burn stick,
Stick will beat dog,
Dog will bite pig,
The pig will jump over the stile,
And we shall get home tonight."
But would the horse drink the water?

IT WOULD NOT.

'Bother, bother, bother!' said the old woman.
Next her tired old feet took her to a farm
where she met a farmer.

"Please farmer," she said,
"Harness horse,
Then horse will drink water,
Water will quench fire,
Fire will burn stick,
Stick will beat dog,
Dog will bite pig,
The pig will jump over the stile,
And we shall get home tonight."
But would the farmer harness the horse?

HE WOULD NOT.

"I'll teach him a lesson," said the old woman crossly. She found a rope hanging over a wall.

"Please rope," she said, "whip farmer,
Then farmer will harness horse,
Horse will drink water,
Water will quench fire,
Fire will burn stick,
Stick will beat dog,
Dog will bite pig,
The pig will jump over the stile,
And we shall get home tonight."
But would the rope whip the farmer?

IT WOULD NOT.

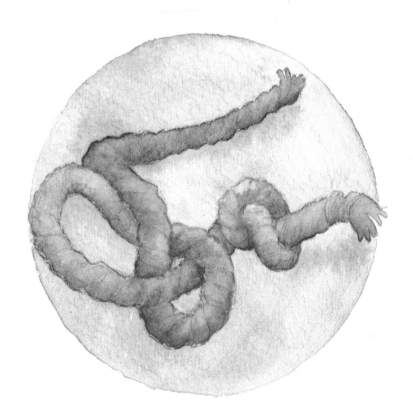

"My patience is wearing very thin,"
grumbled the old woman.
She heard a rat rustling and scuffling in an old barn.

"Please rat," she said,
"Won't you gnaw rope,
Then rope will whip farmer,
Farmer will harness horse,
Horse will drink water,
Water will quench fire,
Fire will burn stick,
Stick will beat dog,
Dog will bite pig,
The pig will jump over the stile,
And we shall get home tonight."
But would the rat gnaw the rope?

HE WOULD NOT.

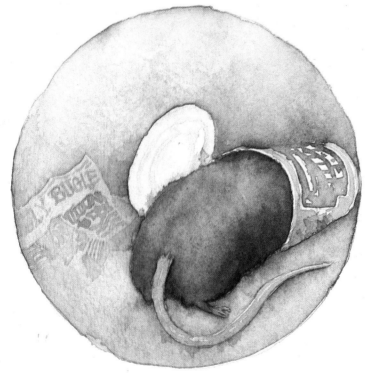

"Good riddance," said the old woman, then she jumped
in surprise when a ginger cat appeared at her feet.

Taking a deep breath, she started,
"Please cat, chase rat,
Then rat will . . ."
"Yes, yes," said the cat,
"I heard it all the first time."
He sat up and stretched.
"How about a large bowl of milk,
Then perhaps . . ."

Suddenly the old woman's feet didn't hurt any more.
She jumped up and danced a jig.

Off she ran to fetch some milk.
"Half now and half when the job's done,"
she said, knowing a thing or two
about cats. So it was agreed.

AND THEN . . .

The cat chased the rat

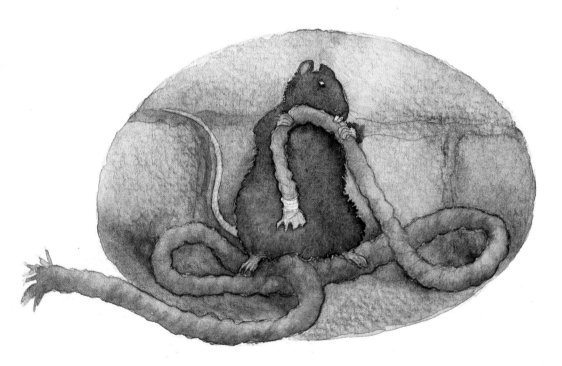

The rat gnawed the rope

The rope whipped the farmer

The farmer harnessed the horse

The horse drank the water

The water quenched the fire

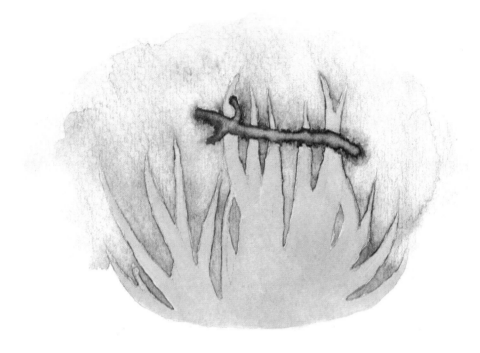

The fire burned the stick

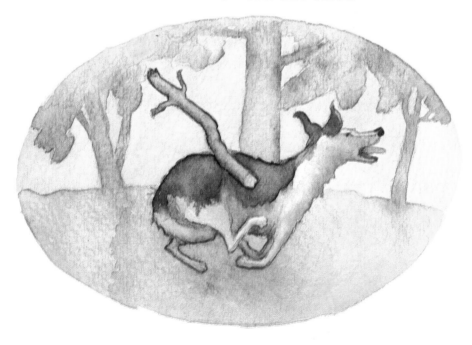

The stick beat the dog

The dog bit the pig

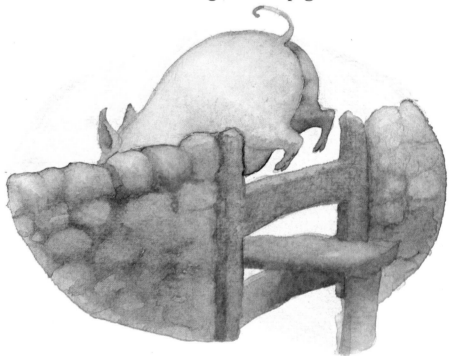

The pig jumped over the stile.

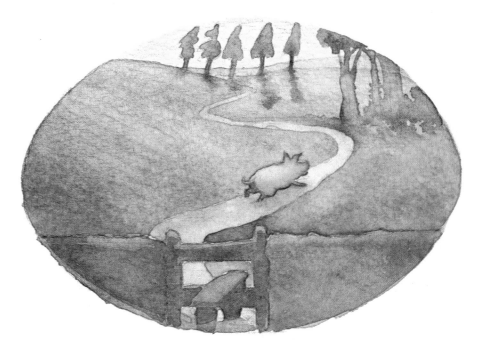

But the pig kept on running

And the old woman had to run after him
Until the sun was down and the moon was up.

At last they had run all the way home, and
they were both so tired that they fell fast asleep,
without any supper at all.